THE
HELIX DEVELOPMENT

THE
HELIX DEVELOPMENT

THE INITIAL CONFLICT

HANNAH BOULD

authorHOUSE®

AuthorHouse™ UK Ltd.
1663 Liberty Drive
Bloomington, IN 47403 USA
www.authorhouse.co.uk
Phone: 0800.197.4150

Published by AuthorHouse   11/19/2013

ISBN: 978-1-4918-8557-4 (sc)
ISBN: 978-1-4918-8562-8 (e)

PROLOGUE

This book is based on the vivid, colourful dreams I have had over the course of the past few weeks. They were in amazing Technicolor, which I think would befit a film rather than a book, as I think the expression of colour and fierce quick action would suit the amazing effects some science fiction films have in place today. It has been my plan to share the results to enable readers to develop their own visual interpretation.

The plot is simple enough to start. A group of three village teenage lads and a tomboy come across a young, frightened eight-year-old girl. The story takes a sinister turn when they discover her farmer father has inadvertently developed a rather primitive machine that makes their lives hell. They try to evade and destroy the machine, not banking on rebellion or personal revenge. Everything escalates into something never experienced by the human race—the unleashed power of the machine. Human greed, hatred, and revenge serve to bring the human race to an ultimatum: infinite combat—a fight to see if science, love, or destruction will prevail. The fact that the machine had one vital flaw has altered the laws of science. No one could see it coming.

Can human nature survive its own apocalypse?

CHAPTER ONE

FRIENDSHIP

◄○►

A young girl, no more than eight or nine years of age, sat on the steps of the village hall. It was a quiet main road. Dressed in boys' dungarees over a light blue shirt, she was slight of build. If it weren't for her long, glossy black hair, prominent blue eyes, and beautiful pale skin, she could have passed for a young boy. She was confused, tired, and hungry. Tears were rolling down her face. She was not able to think further than these steps. She wanted Bruce's fur to snuggle into. Bruce was her Collie dog, her best friend. That was all she could remember. She envisaged him in her mind. Bruce loved her, and he often let her into his basket by the fire. She wondered to herself where home was. She could almost smell Bruce's weird pungent dog smell that was strangely comforting. It was, she thought, also disgusting. The thought made her giggle. She closed her eyes and saw him in the farmhouse, shaking himself free of rain and mud. He always managed to cover her in streaks of wet mud. She saw a man, laughing and mopping her clothes off. "How do I know him? Is he my father? Where is my mother?" she said, although she did not realise she was speaking out loud. Her head was spinning with images, intermingled with memory loss.

Down the road, a small group of friends, happily laughing and chatting, were walking towards the village hall. Three boys and one girl, all home from Sixth Form College and full of camaraderie. Rosie, the oldest at eighteen, was the definite leader of the pack. The three boys, Cameron, Chris, and Matt (all seventeen), were forever trying to entertain her, tease each other, and vie for her attention. All three of them doted on her, as they had all missed her so much. Cameron and Chris had gone off to study maths and physics. Matt was in the same college as them but was concentrating on a career in theatre. Rosie didn't have a clue how beautiful she was. She was incredibly clever and had gone to train at a college in a different town, doing maths, chemistry, and biology. She wanted to be a vet. Tall and slim with long, soft bronze curls, large hazel eyes, pale skin, and a dazzling smile, boys asked her out a lot. With these three boys, she felt very much one of them, and she was fiercely loyal. These were her best friends. She felt none of the awkwardness of teenage anxieties or insecurity she felt around other boys. They were all good looking, from well-to-do families, and very intelligent. They bounced off each other. It was good to be home, Rosie smiled to herself. She was proud of all of them, but the boys' whit sometimes drove her crazy. One silly grin or a nudge made her forgive them every time, though. Boys would be boys. They were all chatting animatedly about things that had happened at college. Cameron and Chris had managed to make the college football team. Both boasted about assists and curls to the back of the net and discussed dirty tackles and how unfair it was when the coach had taken them both off in the last game.

"You know what? Chris and I had scored three times, I hit the net and the keeper went down."

He was talking so fast and with passion that Rosie drifted off into her own thoughts: *Football, again!*

Still, Cameron continued, "Next I managed to pass the ball through the legs of the big defender. Then, as another two defenders ran at me, I passed it back. Chris scored an *amazing* goal. In the beginning of the second half, I managed to run past all three defenders with my skills and shot the ball right in to the top right corner."

Matt had listened intently. He loved football and remembered playing years ago in primary school, then secondary school with Cameron and Chris. They had always been a force to reckon with, even at the age of ten. He felt a twinge of jealousy. His college colleagues were all more artistic and saw football as a mug's game. To get wet and muddy or even injured? No, thank you! Matt had reluctantly conformed to their way. He needed to fit in. He loved getting home after a day at college to spend time these guys. Both he and Chris were slightly quiet, retiring types on their own, but coupled with Cameron, they found another layer and became a little eccentric and loud—to say the least. Rosie was a calming influence on them when they listened! She watched them as they were walking. Not one of them could stop gesticulating with his arms, pretending to show off a free kick or suddenly break into some weirdly annoying song. She knew they spent hours on the computers gaming with each other and had little things they shared. She felt a little excluded, but she had no interest in gaming at all. She preferred to read. The boys had grown up with Rosie. Her mum was one of the coolest in the village. She would often rustle up dinner for the four when they traipsed back from wherever they had been. Rosie had a wicked sense of humour, and she tolerated them for so long before casting some aspersion as to their sanity. She would mimic them, perfecting their accents and mannerisms. No matter how often she did it, the boys couldn't help but dissolve into laughter.

The boys were frivolous and spirited to be together this weekend, so they did not notice the little girl on the steps of the village hall. Rosie did, though, and hastened forward. She knelt beside the dark-haired, fragile girl, whose face was wet with tears. The boys nodded as they saw Rosie move, but pretended not to notice and started kicking a stone to each other on the road. That was girl's business!

"Hi, I'm Rosie. Are you okay?"

The little girl shook her head, she could barely speak. "I can't remember," she managed to whisper. "I can't remember how to get home." Something about Rosie's soft approach let the girl trust her.

Rosie asked, "What's your name?"

"I don't know," sobbed the little girl.

Rosie decided to get the boys' attention. She told them to go ahead to her house and let her mum know they were coming back for dinner with an extra person. The boys, obviously relieved to leave, jogged off laughing to each other about some random subject, as they were often known to do. The boys knew Rosie's mum would welcome them as ever.

"You look hungry and tired," Rosie said, being as gentle as she could. The girl's eyes showed fear. The girl nodded. "Well, I only live down the road. We can get you some food, and you can rest. My mum's a great cook, and you can borrow some of my sister's clothes. She was about the same size as you. We can then set about getting you home." Rosie was calm but persuasive. Her own little sister had been killed in a terrible car accident just a year ago. She hadn't come to terms with it yet. She needed to help this girl. The girl wasn't used to other people, but her hunger overpowered any of her doubts. They set off towards Rosie's home.

Her mum had been as inviting as ever. She always managed to procure enough food for them, always accommodating the needs of three hungry teenage boys. She often watched them, joking and sharing stories. She was just happy that Rosie had such faithful friends. She didn't question Rosie on the sudden appearance of the young girl. She was so thin and obviously exhausted. She left them to eat. Although it was painful, Rosie's mum headed up to Charlotte's bedroom. It was still the same. Typical pinks and soft whites, the teddy bears were still stacked at the foot of the bed. Charlotte had positioned them every night. They had each had names, and she talked to them and told them bedtime stories. Rosie's mum felt something right inside her, letting this little fragile girl settle into this bed.

She patted the bed, "Charlie, we love you and miss you. Tonight, you beautiful little girl, you cannot be with us, but we hope you are looking down from heaven and understand that we have to help this little one. Your sister brought her home, and you know what she is like sometimes!" She felt better for talking out loud. She smoothed the bed sheets out, put the bedside lamp on, and took Charlie's soft, fluffy pink and white dressing gown out of the wardrobe. It was her little princess's room.

In the kitchen, the little girl who came home with Rosie, whilst ravenously stuffing herself with hot chicken and ham pie, nervously tried to explain. "I keep seeing a man in an old farm shed and pictures of a tall, beautiful woman with long, shiny black hair in my head."

She thought the woman may be her mother, but decided not to mention that. After all, she was with a group of strangers. The boys weren't really dealing with the whole situation. Rosie's mum stepped in. The girl was very tired. "Rosie, this young lady needs some sleep. I will take her for a bath and bed."

Rosie said to the girl, "My mum is the best. She will look after you, okay? Trust her." The little girl was wary, but she was enjoying the people around her. It seemed like a long time since she had felt this happy. Rosie's mum, Claire, took her upstairs. She had run a bath, just like she used to for Charlotte. The bath was comforting and warm. Claire left her in peace, but laid some sweet smelling bed clothes out on the radiator. The young girl picked up Rosie's' sister's fluffy dressing gown after drying off and realised how tired she felt. She wasn't sure what to do next. She called Rosie's name downstairs from the landing. Rosie heard her, almost wishing it were Charlotte. She ran upstairs.

The girl said, "I don't know what to do. I'm tired." Rosie saw just how tired the young girl was and took her across the landing into Charlotte's room. Her mother had told her in a whisper that she had set up her sister's room. She spoke softly to this girl, understanding she needed nothing but comfort. She couldn't help but wonder who she was. She settled her in to her sister's bed, deeply feeling the ache of loss. Her heart was struggling.

"I wish you had gotten to meet my sister, Charlie," Rosie told the girl. "I will wake you tomorrow, and we will hunt for your home." The girl was already drifting off to sleep. She smiled inadvertently and was already settling in. Bruce was prominent in her mind, as she felt safe with him. The little girl was fast asleep in seconds. As Rosie sat and watched her, she longed for her younger sister. She sat for ages, watching the girl breathing gently but turning often. She must have been dreaming, and she cried out a few times. Rosie left her to her dreams after folding the quilt on the bed. Just touching the bedsheets and sitting in her sister's room made her feel closer to her.

Rosie went back downstairs. She chatted with the boys, who were all sitting on the big and comfortable worn brown leather sofa while watching the warm glow and flickering flames gently caress the logs. She sat down next to them on the hearth rug. Rosie persuaded the boys to take part in a plan before they all left for the evening. "She must be from somewhere nearby. She mentioned a farm shed and a farm dog. Let's meet tomorrow morning and take her around the farms on the outskirts of the village to see if we can jog her memory." The boys were keen for adventure. Their village, Madeley, provided limited options for young people. They had been at college for a year and aspired to great things. Rosie was already ahead of them. She knew her future, or so she thought.

"Sounds like a plan!" Cameron, who was already standing, said. Rosie stood up next to him.

"Remember that man who lives on Gate Farm? You know, the recluse who no one sees or really knows? No one goes there anymore? A few people have apparently disappeared when they've gone there, or so my mum said," Matt blurted out. He was worried because that was one of the three farms around the village. They had been conditioned by their parents. That farm was definitely one he didn't want to go near.

Rosie was persuasive. She had lost Charlie, and she felt a need inside to help the girl. She was a sister, and she understood the bond between siblings. "Matt, that was just an old wives' tale to stop us wandering when we were kids. Come on! You seriously aren't afraid of some senile farmer?" she mocked.

"She doesn't live there, and there is no way I am going there!" Cameron said. Chris nodded in agreement.

Rosie shook her head, "We will just go to the edge of all the farms. We don't have to go in. Just anything that might help; otherwise, she will have to go to the police station, and I think she is scared enough." She paused and looked into the fire, wondering where on earth this girl had come from. She had lived in the village her whole life and knew almost every one by face or name. She didn't know this young girl. "We have to help her, boys. What would you do if it were my little sister?" They all murmured assent and nodded. All three boys headed out into the dark street, having said their good evenings and thanks to Rosie's mother. The village was strange. It was tiny and about ten miles from the nearest town. It was quite self-sufficient. The villagers had held a meeting a few years prior and decided to avoid street lighting in an effort to be ecofriendly. Much of the produce in the village was grown locally by the three farms. Meat and milk were produced nearby, too. Many of the villagers made their own bread, confectionary, and jams. Despite all this, it was modern in many ways, and the community was close-knit. The boys were used to walking in the dark, but tonight they were silent on the way home.

The following morning, the girl woke much refreshed. With utmost politeness, she thanked Rosie's mum for her hospitality in a manner beyond her years. She apologised for encroaching on them and said how lovely their house was. She had dressed in Charlotte's elegant purple and silver dress, which Rosie's mother had laid out for her. She felt beautiful for the first time in her life. She also saw a glimpse of her mother's face in the mirror, which made her feel good.

Rosie explained their plan over breakfast. "We are going to head out around the village to see if we can jolt your memory, okay?" The girl agreed instantly. She still couldn't remember her name or her home—only little snippets of who she guessed were her parents. And then there was Bruce, gorgeous Bruce. He was the most prominent picture in her mind. She still trusted Rosie. She couldn't quite comprehend her feelings as she was so young. She happily went after breakfast to meet the three boys.

Despite being apprehensive, the boys put up their usual show of joking, messing about, and entertaining. Rosie was used to it. She just rolled her eyes at their antics. The little girl, however, was giggling and totally taken by them.

After visiting two of the three of the farms on the outskirts of the village, the girl was still not remembering anything. They walked farther out of the village, off the main road down a worn track that was overgrown with weeds. The hedges encroached onto the path, loaded with honeysuckle.

Despite the sight and smells, Matt saw the sign ahead and shuddered. Ever since he was little, his parents had always warned him not to go down here. He couldn't help feel the same apprehension he had felt the previous evening. "This is Gate Farm," he said to the girl, and a vague flicker went across her face.

As always, Rosie was confident. Brusquely, she commanded them. "We will just go until we can see the farm. We don't need to go any farther," she said, sensing how uneasy the boys were. She was just as scared, but she felt it was important to continue. She strode forward, taking the little girl's hand. The rest felt they had to follow. "Don't worry!" She tried to relax. They all pretended not to read the sign that said, "DO NOT TRESPASS. PRIVATE PROPERTY. GUARD DOG," painted very boldly in red underneath the farm sign.

A beautiful old farmhouse stood majestically before them at the end of a long drive. It had obviously been a prominent estate at some point, but had lapsed into a degree of disrepair. It was a huge white building, with pillars at the front door. The paint was peeling, though, and ivy was growing up over the windows. The garden in front was overgrown, but had gates and lion statues leading into a small orchard. Damsons, apples, and pears were heavy on the trees.

An old red and white collie dog was rolling on the grass. It looked harmless enough, so they walked down the drive. The collie bound towards them. All of them froze, but he was wagging his tail. He jumped up at the little girl, licking her face.

"Bruce! Bruce!" she exclaimed. Rosie exchanged a look with the boys, trying to hide surprise and anxiousness. The old dog clearly knew this girl. "Come on. Let's see if we can find someone who can talk that recognises you," Rosie laughed.

"Are you sure?" Cameron asked. "I mean, this is quite a way out of the village for her to have come from." He wasn't happy. Matt had not spoken a word, and even Chris, a young man of few words, stayed even more silent than usual.

The little girl spoke up, weirdly mature for her age. "I am sure. Thank you for helping me. I'm still not really sure who I am or what has happened, but this feels like my home." She expressed an edge of confidence that seemed out of place.

"We can't let you just wander in there as though nothing has happened. You can't be sure you know this is your home if you still can't remember your name!" Chris interrupted. He was a very intelligent, well-mannered, well-spoken young man. "I will come with you," he said.

Cameron, Matt, and Rosie said at once, "We *all* will." Bruce ran around them in circles, almost herding them as was his nature.

As they walked into the farmyard, they couldn't help but notice that it was very clean and quiet, despite being run down. The girl ran to the small shed next to the hay barn and opened the door before the others could stop her.

"Megan, my darling!" A voice of delight was heard. The four teenagers headed through the door, just in time to see a middle-aged man scoop the girl into his arms while beaming. "Megan, where have you been? I've been so worried about you! What on earth are you wearing?" barely pausing for breath. He looked up and tried to mask a look of horror and anger, "Who have you brought home with you?"

Rosie, sensing that the atmosphere was unusually tense, replied, "Your daughter was lost. We have just helped her find her way home. I'm really sorry, but she was so tired and hungry last night that by the time she had eaten, she fell asleep. It was too dark to venture out. We didn't know what else to do, but she stayed safely at our house," she spoke too fast. Taking a breath, she said, "I imagine you were so worried." The farmed glared at her.

"Hey," grinned Matt, "Megan, that's a beautiful name!"

Cameron interjected, "I bet you are happy to be home, Megan!"

Chris laughed nervously, "At least we know your name."

The farmer forced himself to relax his shoulders. He did not like strangers here. "Well, my little munchkin, say thank you, and we will let these kind young people go home."

Rosie looked at Megan, "You can keep the dress. You look lovely."

"Daddy, these are my best ever friends!" She had the prettiest smile to go with the bright blue eyes. "Please, Daddy, can they stay for while?" The farmer did not look remotely happy but agreed. He was wary of anyone on his farm, but they were only kids, and they had brought Megan home. They would go soon enough.

"All right, Megan. I guess so. I'll make us all a drink and bring some biscuits. You all sit down here." He gestured to the hay bales. His tone was firm, and they did as they were told.

Sitting on the bales of hay, Megan chattered to the boys excitedly about her time at Rosie's house—how beautiful the bedroom was, the soft fluffy pink dressing gown, the soft white bed sheets, and all the teddies on the chair. She obviously didn't have these sorts of things herself. Rosie looked around. All three boys fawned on Megan, just like they used to with Rosie's younger sister. The shed was small, dark, and dusty. Rosie couldn't help notice a few small golden brown cocoons sitting on a wooden shelf. They looked beautiful. Even in the poor light, they seemed to emit a warm glow. In the corner was an old, large, dark wooden wardrobe. Rosie thought it was a strange place to put a wardrobe, but quickly put it out of her mind. She wanted to get out of there.

"Megan, it's lovely you are home." She stayed as calm as she could. The boys had all relaxed, whereas she started to feel tense. "We can't stay long, but we can ask your father if he would let you come to visit us again. My mother would like that." Megan beamed again.

The farmer came back in with a wooden tray and four large mugs of hot tea. "Could you please get me a bale down, young men?" he motioned, pointing to the far edge of the shed. Chris and Matt stood up and went to get the bale. It was quite high up, so they called Cameron to help lift it down. All the boys were at that tall, skinny gangly age. Matt had never lifted hay bales before. It did require a certain knack, after all. Chris lived in a large house attached to a small Abbey with grounds, a working farm and a fishery. Although his parents had nothing to do with the farm, he spent some of his spare time helping.

The farmer couldn't help but smile. "Come on, lads. I can lift two of those at a time on my own!" He placed the tea tray on one of the bales the boys had been sitting on. He turned his back on Rosie and Megan, walking towards the wardrobe while muttering to himself about sugar. Megan was watching the boys, laughing at their efforts to move the hay bale. Rosie was wandering why the farmer had brought only four mugs of tea.

Without a second to blink, there was a large flash of blinding light and a loud bang. Smoke filled the shed. Rosie jumped. With all the smoke, she ran for the door, which was inches from her. She couldn't see the boys or Megan, but her instinct was to get out. Surely, everyone would be right behind her. She sensed something was wrong. What had happened? Her mind raced. Sure enough, before she got thought the door, she hesitated. She turned around to look for her friends. Another flash of light exploded across the shed, and she felt herself being thrown backward. As she lost consciousness, she heard someone screaming very loudly. Megan.

As Rosie came to her senses, she tried to focus her surroundings in the smoke. Everything looked weird, out of proportion. She felt very dizzy. *I must have hit my head*, she thought, touching her head automatically. She checked her fingers, saw no blood, and figured she'd better stay on the ground. She knew instinctively not to try to move. For what seemed like an eternity, she was too disoriented to think further than that. In the back of her mind, she could hear sobbing now.

"Megan!" she cried out, but she didn't hear a response. The noise was coming from beneath her.

"Rosie, Rosie?" whispered Matt. "Are you alright?" She heard him right next to her and managed to focus close enough to see him but blurrily.

"Yes, I think so" she replied, "Where are Chris and Cameron? Are they okay? What happened? Where are Megan and her father?" She tried to sit up, but felt searing pain throughout her body.

CHAPTER TWO
THE MACHINE

◄○►

"Just stay still and quiet, Rosie. We have been trapped. Chris and Cameron are here, too. I think we got hit by a blast before you." Matt was firm and spoke quietly. "It's not good. It may be that we have been poisoned and are delusional, though how all four of us could have been is beyond me. We didn't have any of that tea. We felt a thud and saw a bright light that seemed to knocked us over. Now we are in some kind of metal cage, and well, I don't want to believe it," he said. He wasn't really explaining himself—more talking out loud to try to make sense of what had just happened.

"Just say it, Matt!" said Chris.

Before Matt could speak again, Cameron burst out "We have been shrunk, I think!" They looked at each other, shocked with the sudden realisation of the actual predicament they were in. Rosie, just coming out of the fog, peered below. They were suspended in some kind of, well, she could describe it only as bird cage. It reminded her of the one her grandmother had with a beautiful orange canary in it. He sang constantly. She had often wondered if he was singing for a mate or for freedom. She had always felt sorry for him. She now understood how he must have felt. Panic started to set in. What would happen to them? She, too, had heard tales of people never returning from this farm. Her parents had mentioned it in passing a few years back. She felt sick. She couldn't help but wondering what those cocoons on the wooden rail were. She glanced at the boys. The three of them were used to her guidance, and she realised she had to take control.

"Boys, we need to find a way out, but I think we need to hear what that man is saying to his daughter. It may help us. Stay quiet." By speaking firmly and softly, she provided a good calming influence. Despite their predicament, they all visibly relaxed. Moments before, Matt's eyes had been wide with fear, and Chris had gone even more pale than normal. Cameron had been gripping his hands tightly together, his knuckles taut with fear and anger. He had a fiery temper, and he was watching the farmer's every tiny hand gesture. If he weren't imprisoned, he'd be turning that monster of a man into a midget too.

As the four moved closer to the edge of the cage, it moved ever so slightly and caught the farmer's eye. They lay as still as they could. They would still be disoriented, he rationalised; his main concern was calming Megan. He turned back and continued talking softly to his daughter. Megan was still sobbing quietly, utterly afraid but couldn't quite comprehend the situation. She knew everything that had just happened was wrong, but her father loved her. He must have done it for a reason. He explained as gently as he could, with soothing words. "My darling child, don't worry. I have a very big thing to explain to you. I need you to listen and trust me as your father." Megan nodded, and he took her up onto his lap. She tried to relax but was all too aware of her newfound friends. Where were they? Possibly dead?

"Okay, my child. I have been working on this machine since your mother died. It has helped us keep the farm and have enough money and food to live." He looked fondly into her eyes. She struggled, but smiled back. Somehow, she knew deep down she had to play the role, probably subconsciously, but she snuggled into his arms.

"Daddy, I was so scared when I wasn't here with you. I got so frightened, and I couldn't remember how to get home. I just kept thinking about Bruce. I am so glad to be home with you."

"Don't worry, my pet. You are safe again now. Those people came to steal our machine. They tricked you. When I have tucked you into bed, I will contact the police. Megan, the police will deal with them. You, my darling, are now old enough to learn about this machine?" Rosie thought his tone was very persuasive, but she motioned to the boys to remain quiet a little longer. They all continued listening.

The farmer continued, "Megan, since your mother died when you were a baby, I have worked as hard as I could. I missed your mother so much, and I began tinkering with some machinery. I managed to design a machine that could help us and provide for us. If I had one carrot, it could make 100 carrots. The same with anything, I can make more cows, sheep, food—anything we need. I didn't have space for more animals or stores of food. I know this is probably confusing, but I managed to get the machine to shrink anything, so I could store one hundred carrots in a matchbox. If our cows and sheep are miniature, in tiny pens, they only need tiny amounts of food. When I needed to sell them, I could make them normal-sized to sell. I trust you now, my little princess, to join me in running the farm. If this machine got into the wrong hands, people would use it for bad things. They could make money and armies and all sorts of things. I had to protect you and me tonight. Those people could have ruined our lives." The farmer looked over at the cocoons and smiled to himself.

They were still safe, and he had his little girl back to help him run the farm. Megan reminded him of his wife, with her features, confidence, and laughter. He couldn't stand to lose Megan, ever.

He took her around the farm, showing her the creations he had managed to keep secret from her for years. She couldn't help but be in awe of the tiny creatures. She started to remember how happy she had always been at home and nearly forgot what had just happened.

The farmer sensed that his daughter had been through too much, and he loved her so dearly. "Megan, I think an early dinner and bedtime is what you need. Let's take you into the kitchen, and you can give Bruce a stroke whilst I rustle you up some tea. In the morning, I will show you how to feed our cows. Doesn't that sound lovely?" Megan was hungry and tired, and her father's voice lulled her, as did the thought of snuggling up to their sheepdog. The farmer ambled across the yard and into the house, with Megan still in his arms. A warm kitchen, with a lit stove, was welcome enough. She saw Bruce in his basket and slid out of her father's arms to nestle in Bruce's bed. He was so happy to see her. He licked her face and wagged his tail and then moved to let her fit next to him.

Meanwhile, Rosie and the boys had spent the better part of an hour trying to find their way out of the bird cage. Rosie explained to the boys, "If he can reverse shrinking of his food and animals, we need to get out of this cage and work out how to do that to ourselves." The boys tried the door on the cage. "I know my grandma has arthritis, but she can still unhook the door for her canary." Rosie was pushing them, and she knew she was pushing the right buttons, even in the midst of this awful predicament.

Chris and Matt managed to scale the bars, "Thank goodness for wall climbing in the holidays," Chris said to Matt. He was a natural, being smaller and more nimble, and he reached the door of the cage.

Rosie and Cameron stood and watched. "Be as quiet as you can. We have no idea where that evil man is," Rosie whispered. Cameron wanted to help, but he was afraid of heights. He felt completely out of his element. Rosie was his friend, and for some reason, he felt he needed to help free Megan, as well. But he didn't know how.

Chris, however, was thinking more about the machine. He was imagining what he could do with it and how much money he could make. He mentioned this quietly to Matt, and the duo realised their thoughts were the same. They were both keen to develop their life and work skills, but they just hadn't narrowed it down as far as Rosie had. Cameron was a wild card.

Megan was woken by her father from the warm, familiar smell of Bruce's bed. She ate stew and crusty bread and then gratefully curled up in her own bed. She forgot instantly Rosie's sister's bedroom. Meanwhile, Megan's father was smiling and content, as he had his little girl back again. He sat back in his chair, with a glass of whisky and a cigar. A rare treat. He felt no need to check on the kids he'd imprisoned. They weren't going anywhere until he cocooned them tomorrow, and he would tell Megan that they had escaped. He fell asleep happy.

Rosie and the boys managed to open the bird cage. It had taken all of their strength to push the door open. They climbed down carefully and hid among the hay bales. They were desperately tired, but at only four inches high, they realised they were better off staying put. Matt suggested that they try to activate the machine to make themselves normal again. Cameron said it was too risky that late at night. "Let's sleep and stay hidden tonight." He was right—they needed rest.

Rosie agreed, "We have no idea if this will work. We are in danger, and we also have to save Megan. Let us sit tight tonight and wait. Our folks know we are teenagers, so they will think we are all at an impromptu party away for the night." Again, Rosie was in control.

Megan woke up late in the night. She was a little confused, and she felt a need to check her friends. After all, they had reunited her with her father. She knew nothing of the machine before tonight, so how could they? No one ever came to the farm, and she had no other friends. She clambered out of bed and snuck out to the shed after dressing. Entering the barn, she called softly," It's me, Megan. Are you okay?"

Carefully, Chris and Matt stuck their heads out. "Hey, Megan! We are here over here." Cameron and Rosie stood up.

"Please, we didn't come to steal anything. We only came to bring you home," explained Cameron. Matt and Chris nodded. "Please, Megan. We need your help," said Matt.

"Can you try to work your dad's machine for us?" said Chris. "We had no idea this was here. We just wanted to get you home safely." Rosie didn't speak, for she knew the boys had this. Megan looked in wonderment. Her friends were tiny. She adored them all, so she helped them climb down. Rosie started to figure out the machine once Megan lifted her on to it. With Rosie's help and guidance, Megan managed to work out how to convert them back to normal size. However, none of them considered that the light and noise generated would wake Megan's father.

"Megan, we didn't even know about this machine. Thank you for trusting us," Matt said. Megan looked and felt a little overwhelmed by the events of the past couple of days. For a young child, her world had turned topsy-turvy, but inside, she felt there was something still wrong or missing.

The farmer woke at the noise and jumped from his chair, instinctively calling Bruce to his side. He hated intruders. They all ended up cocooned in his storeroom. It was such an effort, though. Why couldn't people just leave him and Megan be? One day, she would take over this farm. She had seen the machine, now from a child's eyes, rather than the sixteen year old he had tried to show yesterday. Megan would make the farm so great that it would keep them both wealthy, warm, and fed. His wife would have been proud. He went towards the barn, and as he entered, he saw Megan and protectively scooped her up.

"Baby, what on earth are you doing in here so late? Back to bed!" In his hesitation, picking her up and worrying, as well as being a little tipsy, he failed to notice that Chris was standing next to the machine in the wardrobe. Chris aimed and pressed a button. He had no idea what would happen, but it seemed like an idea at the time. He only knew that the man was no good. Before them, a strange thing started to happen. The shapes of the farmer and Megan seemed to change, but not shrink. They started almost moulding into wax. Matt, Cameron, Rosie, and Chris stared as the farmer became an older woman and Megan transformed into a little boy. Something in Rosie's head made her instinctively grab the young boy Megan had become and pull him to her. Chris pulled a lever on the machine, and a blast of blue light lit up the shed. The farmer, now a woman, had shrunk to a height of four inches and looked a little confused. Cameron had been quite taken by all the events, and as intelligent as he was, he needed answers. He was one for analysing things in his head. This was a very different situation, and yet for some reason, he found it exciting. Ignoring Rosie, Matt, and Chris, who were all talking to the young boy, he stepped over and picked up the farmer.

"Why have you done this?" he asked. "I will reverse the machine if you tell me how, but then I will destroy it." Cameron was furious. "You can't play with lives like this."

The farmer nodded, for he wasn't exactly in a place to argue. It was hard to hear because the farmer was so small, but Cameron listened intently. The farmer seemed to collect his thoughts, which took what seemed like forever. Eventually he spoke. "When I lost Megan's mother, I started building this machine, just as something to do. I managed to slow the growth of the animals so I could sell them as younger meat for better money. I then managed to develop it to reverse age, so that older animals became young again. With more time, I managed to get the machine to multiply and shrink items. It is an amazing machine. It has given Megan and me a life with money to live on. I nearly lost Megan. She was a beautiful child. She grew up and lost interest in the farm, spending more time in the village. I couldn't help it. I couldn't lose her! She has to be the one to take over our farm." He stopped.

"What do you mean she grew up? She is only eight!" Cameron was still angry.

The farmer continued reluctantly, but he was also scared. Cameron was towering above him, and the farmer could see he could not get past him or to the machine. "Megan isn't eight. She's nearly seventeen. She questioned the machine yesterday. I had shown it to her, thinking she would be excited. I tried to explain what it was for. She argued that it was unnatural and wrong. I just pressed the button. She was my little girl again. It obviously interfered with her memory. She ran off. I couldn't exactly call the police. I had been out looking for her until late last night. You brought her back to me today. I need her to carry on with our farm when I get too old. She has to stay here and not be sucked in to the village and boys. A few people have been too nosy, and I couldn't let them talk. Hence, they are shrunk in cocoons until there is a day where Megan can run the farm, and they have forgotten. I have been tinkering with this machine ever since. I didn't initially realise its capabilities. The reducing action was accidental, but it helped so I could produce a carrot, shrink it, and have 100 carrots. I then reversed it and could sell 100 young, sweet-tasting carrots at the market. I could make sheep and cows young again, which is better for the meat market. I also managed to change the sex of the animals—females bring in milk and more offspring. But I needed a few males to ensure reproduction, so I converted some of the older females into males, which meant bigger hides, more meat, and more financial gain. My only failure has been reducing an animal's age more than once. It doesn't work. So I have my Megan back for now, but not indefinitely." Despite his situation, the farmer could not help talking animatedly about his work.

"What about changing sex more than once? What are the risks in that?" Cameron asked.

"I have never tried it," the farmer replied.

Rosie had been listening carefully. She knew this machine needed to be destroyed, but Megan needed to be her correct age again. "Tell us how to reverse sex, and we will try it on you first," she exclaimed. The farmer, all of a few inches high and currently a woman was not really able to argue and reluctantly explained the procedure.

The farmer asked, "Make me a normal size again?"

Rosie glared, "We will be calling the police, as well, so you will be normal, but I will make sure you can't escape." She too was angry.

They set the machine, successfully transforming the farmer into himself. Rosie deliberately left him tiny and controllable. She turned to the little boy, who was very upset and confused. "Megan, I know a lot has happened today. It's just your dad has a machine that he didn't really understand. He does now, though, and we need you to stand here to let you be you again. I know that sounds weird, but I think you will be okay. Trust me?"

Megan nodded and stepped forward. Chris was getting the hang of the machine. He now knew what to do. Within a few moments, Megan had been transformed into a beautiful young woman of sixteen, with long black sleek hair and the same stunning blue eyes. Cameron recognised her. She had been at a young farmers' disco last year, yet he had never seen her again. He had thought about her for months. His heart melted. One of the side effects was of the machine was temporary memory loss, so Megan had no idea what had just happened. Rosie asked Matt and Chris to tie the farmer up to the cattle shed rails just outside before he was transformed back to his normal size. Cameron was too busy beaming at Megan. Rosie was a little jealous and surprised at her thoughts. He was her friend and nothing more. She shook herself together. They needed to get off the farm and contact the police. "We need to get going, guys. Megan, I know this is hard. I promise to explain, but let's head back to the village." Everyone had been through enough and eager to leave. The farmer looked on, but was completely bewildered due to the transient memory loss.

As they headed back into the village, Megan and Cameron chatted closely. Cameron was trying to remind Megan of the past few days, as well as the fact that she was nearly seventeen rather than eight. The other three moved apart from them.

"We need to destroy that machine," Rosie said to Matt and Chris. She called the police from the nearest telephone box. She told them the Farmer at Gate Farm had tried to kidnap her and her friends (leaving out the shrinking part). She explained that that they had managed to trick him, and had escaped. She sounded breathless. "We are running home, we are scared." Even now Rosie was in control. "We managed to tie him up but I'm sure he will be after us, please?" She cut the line dead and grinned. "I want to know what is in those cocoons. I have a feeling it has something to do with missing people."

Chris piped up, "It's dangerous there. Let's wait until tomorrow. It's so dark now, and hopefully, the police will have taken Megan's father to the station."

Rosie called back to Cameron and Megan; "We will meet at nine am tomorrow. We have to go back now, Megan. You can stay at my house again tonight, though it might confuse my mum a bit! I'll just say I met you as the little girl's older sister when we found her home, and you and I realised we knew each other from college. She won't mind." They were nearly at Rosie's house.

Megan was still recovering from temporary memory loss. Something made her feel it was okay to trust them. She had a warm feeling towards the vivacious blond boy, Cameron, and Rosie seemed so clever. Cameron was telling her things she vaguely recalled.

Matt and Chris had been quietly chatting, both been in awe of the machine and its potential.

Rosie interjected, "No, we need to destroy it, guys. Surely you can see how dangerous it is?" The boys didn't disagree, but you could see the possibilities of the machine were firmly implanted in their minds.

Megan had also heard parts of the conversation and said, "I am angry with my father. I need to speak to him."

Cameron said, "I agree with Rosie, Megan. We need to destroy that machine. It's dangerous, and I'm not sure your father will be in a good frame of mind! We did just shrink him, turn him into a woman, turn him back, and then tie him up for the police!" He not was one to mince his words. Rosie felt unsure, as did Megan. They had been through a lot that day, and it had been weird. Megan asked to be alone for a while. She felt sick and dizzy. After asking her mother, Rosie took Megan upstairs to Charlie's bedroom and left Megan alone with her own thoughts.

As she left, she said, "I'll be back for dinner. Just rest. You've been through too much." Megan was already drifting off to sleep.

Matt and Chris had gone off on their own, but Cameron, anxious about Megan, was waiting outside for Rosie. "Is she okay?" he asked anxiously.

Rosie replied "She's tired. We have no idea how she must feel. We were all shell-shocked from being shrunk. She has been changed to a little girl, then a boy, and then back to her normal age: I would imagine that's like getting hit by a train. Let's go get and chill at the river. It's been a crazy couple of days." Settled down by the bank of the river, Rosie and Cameron were silent, each reflecting on their own thoughts and feelings. Nothing could have prepared them for what had happened. It almost seemed like a dream. Rosie cared for Cameron more than she had realised. Cameron was thinking about how beautiful Megan was. Eventually, Rosie and Cameron started talking. They agreed that they had to find a way of destroying the machine. Both were worried that Megan would get into more harm with her obviously deranged father if the machine weren't destroyed.

Meanwhile, the two police officers had turned up at Gate Farm after Rosie's phone call. They found the farmer tied to a cattle bar talking what seemed to be complete nonsense. The farmer had also briefly lost his memory. They did a scout around the farm and house and found nothing. They checked the shed, but neither of the officers bothered to look inside the wardrobe. When questioned, the farmer had no recollection of the events. He seemed completely bewildered about any mention of anyone having been at the farm. The officers had settled him back into his front room, complaining to each other of an obvious prank from kids wasting their evening. They left, and the farmer soon fell asleep on his chair by the dying embers of the fire.

Chris and Matt had gone off together, as they had more plans. The machine had so many possibilities! In one day, they had seen what it was capable of. Reversing and advancing age, changing sexes, and shrinking and increasing just about anything. They were both a little geeky anyway, so this machine just fascinated them. They formulated a plan to go out to the farm early in the morning, without the others, to try to take the machine. Surely, the farmer would be in custody. It would be a breeze. They simply had to figure what its energy source was. They thought it would be an easy ride. Driven by greed and without any real plan, they decided to meet at dawn the following morning.

Rosie and Cameron headed home from the river. They agreed to meet at dawn to go destroy the machine. Rosie was to check how Megan felt to see if she wanted to go with them. They had decided not to tell Chris or Matt that they were going early. They felt they didn't need to. It was putting more of them in danger, and they had also seen the awe in their eyes over the machine.

What none of them realised was that the farmer had come out of his brief bewilderment. When he awoke, he had figured he had a challenge ahead. He wanted his daughter back, and he knew she would come looking for him. He had gone out to the shed during the night and checked his machine. Everything was intact. He locked the wardrobe doors as a precaution before heading to bed.

Rosie woke very early the next morning and found that Megan was awake too.

"Megan?" whispered Rosie.

"When are we going?" Megan replied.

Rosie seemed a little perplexed, as she hadn't talked to Megan when she got home. "Rosie, you talk in your sleep! When are we going to confront my father?"

Rosie suddenly understood how the little girl she met had seemed so mature for her years. "Megan, you don't have to come. We need to destroy that machine your father built. He can't control you anymore."

Megan replied, "I know it is dangerous, but I want to come with you. My father needs stopping. He isn't the father I know or remember. I think he has gone mad." She was determined to put things right.

CHAPTER THREE
THE CONFRONTATION

The girls dressed hastily, quietly sneaking out of the house. Cameron was waiting for them, and he beamed when they arrived.

"Hey, you girls ready for this?"

Rosie kept finding herself staring as this new woman in front of her. She was strangely jealous. Cameron was obviously smitten. She made herself concentrate. They had a serious task ahead.

Rosie said, "Yes, Cam, Megan and I are very ready." The three of them headed down the lane out of the village. It was eerily quiet, even the bird song was minimal. There was fresh dew on the grassy curb edges and hedges. The beautiful soft dawn light, almost oyster pink and yellow, made the drops of dew glisten. They took it all in, despite was before them that day, and they savoured nature as the most amazing creation of life.

They reached the farmhouse's long drive, and Megan motioned and whispered, "My father should be just milking the cows. When he took me round the farm yesterday, he had the animals all miniature, but he has to make them full-sized long enough to get the milk. I've only ever seen him with normal cows before." She was second guessing herself, but knew she was right. "The problem is that I don't know if he moves his machine. The shed is too small to fit two hundred cows in, and the farm is so clean. Cows aren't clean. We need to head around the farmhouse from the other side. Follow me." It felt strange being given instructions from a girl who had been a child only yesterday, but Rosie and Cameron followed her without hesitation.

Meanwhile, Matt and Chris had been up even earlier. They were already hidden in the shed at the farm amongst the hay bales. The wardrobe doors were shut and locked, which was a complication that hadn't envisioned.

"I don't remember any of the others locking it!" Matt was cautious.

Chris said, "Knowing Rosie, I bet she did. She's so clever and always thinking ahead!" Chris was proud to have her as a friend. They both felt guilty at being here without her. They would have to sit it out until they figured a plan.

"Do you think we can carry it, Chris?" asked Matt.

"Hey, look at us! I am in prime fitness, thanks to my footy coach. Those laps of the field and the press-ups will finally pay off."

Chris replied, laughing. Matt was a very confident young man, a fabulous public speaker. He had most of the girls at college languishing on his every word. No was not a word in his vocabulary. They would succeed. Quietly worried, Matt felt reassured by Chris' words. They sat and discussed what they would do once they had that machine and where they would keep it. Chris' family was very wealthy and had a large house. It was a converted old-people's home with numerous rooms, all very elegantly decorated reflecting taste and money. He was left to himself at home, and his mother barely bothered him. They had numerous outbuildings, as well, storing Indian furniture that his parents shipped in from abroad to sell. He knew some of the buildings stored some of his things whilst he was at college. It would be easy to put the machine in there. Even he was surprised that his old stores of vivaria, all homemade, were still there, dusty and empty. Frogs, snakes, and snails had once been housed in those.

From the woods farther down the lane, Rosie, Cameron, and Megan had come onto the farm from the opposite side, with the farmhouse way over to the left near the long drive. Sure enough, they were right to listen to Megan. The farm buildings were all strangely quiet and clean; there was no stench of muck that normally accompanies cows and sheep. No slurry pit, and no feeding towers. Megan knew where the milking parlour was. As they crept towards it, she could already hear the familiar sound of the pumps being washed and rinsed. They were right on time. Her father would be bringing the cows in shortly. This was the bit she had never seen, as she had rarely been in the milking parlour. Her father used to tell her that some of the cows didn't like being milked and would kick. He told her the story of a farmer hit on the head by a cow's hoof and that he had collapsed in the milking pit and died of a brain haemorrhage. Megan had trusted her father. None of them could guess what would happen now. The plan was for Megan to distract her father whilst Rosie and Cameron found the machine and disconnected the power source before trying to break it. Cameron had already spied a pile of old gates and managed to procure several metal, albeit slightly rusty, poles.

The farmer was getting ready for the morning's milking. The parlour was ready. Having previously scouted the farm and finding all well, he went to the shed to collect his machine. Matt and Chris heard the barn door open and watched quietly. The farmer stood and stared at the wardrobe. He was very proud of it. Despite its basic appearance, the machine inside had kept him and Megan comfortable enough. It wasn't without its flaws, though. It could also reverse age more than once. Megan could still be his little girl again. He was aware that his machine couldn't divide things, but it wasn't necessary for his farm work. It just meant that he could singlehandedly run the farm with minimal costs. He and Megan ate their own produce with no ill effects, so he felt no guilt in selling it for others to consume. Megan would come home, as this farm was her future.

He spoke out loud to himself, "She will see it for what it is soon enough. She is too intelligent to be snared in by mindless college teenagers. She will have seen enough to know what is right." He persuaded himself of this and smiled. His wife would have been proud. Chris and Matt looked at each other in disgust. The farmer looked at the cocoons glowing on the wooden shelf.

Megan had seen her father leave the milking parlour and head towards the shed. She, Rosie, and Cameron snuck into the parlour and hid behind the large milk storage tank. There was a window just above them on the outer wall. Cameron, being the tallest, could just see the barn and the cattle sheds. Matt and Chris saw the farmer unlock the wardrobe and pull out the machine. It was on wheels, something none of the kids had noticed the previous day. Chris noticed it was not plugged into anything—surely it wouldn't work? How could they get the farmer away from it? They needed a distraction. At least it was out of the wardrobe and mobile. They slid down the bales as the farmer pushed the machine towards a barn by the milking parlour. Cameron also saw the farmer and advised the girls. Now was the time to move. He couldn't see any wires or leads, so presumed the machine was currently non-functional just as Chris and Matt had. He knew something so powerful would need a power source.

"I will go first," said Megan firmly. "If my father sees me alone, it doesn't matter, and I can play up to him!" She couldn't help but cock her head to one side and flutter her eyelashes dramatically, grinning. The situation was tense, but she still made Rosie and Cameron laugh.

"We will head over to the barn and see what he is doing," Cameron said. Looking at Rosie, he said, "We will stay low to the ground close to the farm buildings. We can stay out of sight if we go behind there." He motioned towards the corrugated roof at the back of the milking parlour. "We can come around from the other side. The only problem is then getting across the yard." Cameron was using his skills he had learned from hours gaming in battles and hideouts. This was his territory. Rosie just nodded.

Chris and Matt saw Megan because she boldly walked straight out of the milking parlour into the yard. Despite making her jump by whispering to her, she remained as composed as she could.

"Megan, what are you doing here? Are you on your own?" Matt asked.

Without blinking an eye, she said, "Yes, I am here to put things right with my father. I have no one else. I know he won't hurt me. Why are you two here?"

Matt and Chris were a little taken aback. This girl had guts coming back on her own. They were impressed. Before anyone could speak, the sounds of cows eager to have their full udders milked filling the previously silent yard with noise. As Megan had anticipated, full-sized cows were jostling each other to walk across the yard to the parlour.

Megan, standing next to Chris and Matt, saw her father lovingly guide cows to the milking parlour. Bruce was gently at their heels.

Megan's long-term memory was coming back, jolted by these familiar sights and smells. She remembered asking to go to the village and her father always finding excuses. Her father pulled the machine alongside him, disappearing with it into the parlour.

What Megan didn't realise was that her father had never gotten over losing his wife so young, leaving him to bring up a child. Megan turned out to be a strong-willed, intelligent young woman. He worried she would leave him, and there would be no one to run their farm. He saw so many of his late wife's mannerisms and looks in Megan. He loved her dearly.

Megan looked angrily across the farm at her father. *How could my father try to change my life! Manipulate me?* She screamed in her head. *I loved and trusted him. How dare he!* The childlike emotions she had experienced over the past few days were draining away, and she was firmly back to her teenage self. She no longer wanted to destroy the machine—her only thoughts were to destroy her father and the farm. Any conscious rational thoughts had been replaced with rage. The young people were all at an age at which they acted impetuously without the insight that adulthood inevitably brought. Everything seemed possible. Megan felt empowered. "He is no longer my father. He is a monster!" she exclaimed to Chris and Matt. They both looked a little surprised, not quite expecting this. However, they also got the feeling that this girl was a force to reckon with.

She forgot all about Cameron and Rosie, but the original plan still had some sense. "I will distract him. I will pretend I had to come home. Can either of you remember the levers or buttons to shrink him again? If we are lucky, maybe you can do it several times so he is just a particle—dust." There was a steely determination in her voice. The boys nodded. They gulped, as none of them sure what would happen if they failed.

"Megan, what if your father is ready for you?" Matt was really concerned.

"Well, you will just have to figure that out if he does!" Megan scowled at him, but her lips formed a tiny smirk. She was full of adrenaline and ready for anything, not that she had a clue what to do next. She just knew she had to confront him head on.

Megan directed Matt and Chris around the back of the parlour where the cows left after being milked. She walked boldly up to the front of the parlour, calling Bruce. He ran towards her, delighted, and jumped up to greet her. "Good boy," she said as she patted his head and kissed him. He licked her face and sat waiting for her to move. Collies are like that, faithful and almost blinkered when they trust their owners.

Cameron turned, and Rosie had a look of horror on her face. "What on earth is she doing? I just saw Chris and Matt go behind the parlour! Why are they here?" he asked, shocked.

"I didn't tell them we were coming," Rosie whispered angrily back. "Megan was with me all night. So what did you say?"

"Rosie, believe me, I didn't say anything." Cameron remembered the look in their eyes when they had left the farm the previous day. He felt sick to his stomach. Something felt wrong. "This isn't good. We shouldn't have let Megan come. I don't think she is fully recovered from all that has happened. She could get herself and the boys into terrible danger."

Rosie agreed, "I think the poor girl has had more than a few shocks in the last few days! We need to get in there fast." For some reason, the glowing cocoons in the shed came back into her thoughts. There was something else, something more sinister, behind this. She swallowed the bile rising in her throat. "Cameron, when we were shrunk, I managed to work out several of the buttons with Megan. I think I can remember which one shrunk the farmer. If we can get in unseen, we have to get to that machine before anyone else."

Luckily for them, Megan hadn't mentioned to the boys that Cameron and Rosie were with her, such was her anger and focus. She had watched full-sized cows coming from the barn where she had seen miniature replicas proudly presented to her. They looked bewildered, but, as is the nature of cows, they followed each other, habitually heading down into the parlour, waiting their turn.

He subjected me to that. What was I to him, a guinea pig? I'm not just one of his farm animals, she thought angrily. She wanted revenge *now.*

The farmer was busy ticking off the cow brand numbers. The regulations in cattle farming were very strict. Due to outbreaks of foot and mouth disease, restrictions were tight. The last thing he needed was some ministry official snooping around his farm. He was momentarily absorbed by this thought. *Nobody snoops around my farm,* he thought as he smiled.

Megan had only worked out a fraction of what this machine could do. From the edge of the parlour by the door, she could see her father attaching the machine to a large cable leading into the milk storage tank room. She knew she needed the boys' help. She stepped backward from the parlour and went around to join them at the back. The noise of the pumps was loud enough that their conversation was secure.

Megan said, "Can either of you get round the back of the machine without being seen? The old man is distracted filling the chart in. There are still a good number of cows to come through.

He can milk only so many at a time, so we have a good chance." She was so confident.

Matt nodded, "I'm the smallest and fastest. That's why I was always our best striker. Right, Chris?" He tried to joke, but it was all bravado.

"Quit messing. You get behind the machine and try to figure the buttons. I think it was on the far left, the one I hit you all with to make you normal again. So try a different one." She was deadly serious.

"I hit two buttons," Chris reminded her, "One of them changed you and him, um, into the opposite sex, before I managed to shrink him. That was definitely right in the centre, because I panicked and just focused long enough to see it was surrounded by a silver ring."

"Right. Well, Matt, aim for that once you get there and then give us the thumbs up. I'll call Bruce and unsettle the cows. And don't miss! Chris, stay here. We may need you as another diversion. I'm heading back to the front now." She turned and made her way back to the doors. Bruce ran straight to her. Boldly, she stepped right into the doorway. "Bruce, around, around." He was used to this command, but not here, but did as he was told. He motioned forward to try to move the cows on the far side of the parlour. Panic ensued. Most of the cows had suction pumps on their teats and started bucking and kicking frantically. The peaceful early morning milking became a fracas. The pumps were coming off and being trampled, but the cows couldn't get out of the stalls. The farmer panicked, looked round to see Megan standing smirking in the doorway.

"Down, Bruce. Stay!" he bellowed at the dog. Bruce sank to the floor, and he didn't move a muscle again. "What on earth are you doing, Megan? You know how dangerous it is down here in the pit."

He tried to compose himself. After all, his daughter had come back. It was too late.

Matt had managed to climb behind the machine and aimed squarely at the farmer. He looked at the controls, and all thoughts of what they had just discussed left his brain. He couldn't tell what did what!

"Here goes!" he closed his eyes and jabbed his fists onto the machine. Chris, in the meantime, could see that the cows behind Megan were starting to panic and trying to lunge forward into the parlour. He managed to detach the chain attached to the end stall and push it open. The cows pushed into the open yard behind him. They continued to stampede through, but at least there was no pile up. Megan narrowly avoided being knocked over by throwing herself down into the pit. She looked around frantically, but all she could see was a tiny, beautiful golden cocoon. Matt opened one eye and saw Megan in the pit. He could just make out the cocoon, too. They looked at each other.

"Are you okay?" Matt asked.

"I think so," Megan smoothed herself down and shook her hair. "I recognise this. There were some of these in the shed? What are they?" She didn't want to touch it, but had a strange feeling she knew what had happened. She climbed out of the pit, but the old man was nowhere to be seen. He had been cocooned. She stood next to Matt, "What did you press?"

He tried to look serious, but shrugged his shoulders and grinned sheepishly. "I'm sorry, Megan. It isn't every day that I'm asked to shrink wrap someone!"

Rosie and Cameron had seen the light and noise, and they ran into the parlour without regard for their safety. They were worried about their friends. Rosie saw the cocoon, immediately recognising it as being the same as the ones on the wooden shelf in the shed.

It dawned on her very quickly. The reports of people going missing and the stories she had thought were just to scare her. This was what happened to those people. This hadn't yet dawned on the boys, as they never thought about the finer details. None of them had noticed the cocoons in the shed. Megan turned around. She, too, had suddenly realised what that meant—that man had done this to other people! What if one of those cocoons were her mother? She had had a very secluded upbringing. She didn't see many people apart from rare trips into the village. She knew she was expected to marry a farmer and take over from the old man eventually, and she knew her father had wished he'd had a son instead. Her mind began to race. He had tried to steal her life! Selfish old man. He deserved his fate. Her bright blue eyes flashed with anger. Images kept coming into her head—past events, people—all jumbled up.

What no one realised was that this machine was more powerful than any of them could even entertain. Even the farmer hadn't a clue. After all, he had only been trying to find a way of making the farm run smoothly. To be fair, the hours he spent working on it also helped ease the pain of losing his wife. Even when he realised he could use it to reverse age, it didn't dawn on him what he was doing when he needed his little girl back. The machine warped reality and imagination, making tiny changes, mutations deep within the gene code, to DNA. It wasn't enough to be noticed in the short term.

Chris was trying to head the panicking cows away from the long drive. He was used to farming to a small degree, and knew that 200 cows running loose on country lanes was not good. When he had whistled Bruce, the dog was at his side in an instant. This was turning out to the strangest week of his life. Little did he know that this was only the beginning.

Megan turned and saw Rosie, whose face was very pale. Matt was still standing next to Megan by the machine. Without hesitation, she hit a button in front of her, as hard as she could. "Megan, no!" screamed Matt, "What are you doing?" Lights flashed again, and the noise as deafening as before. He could barely see, but Rosie and Cameron were becoming cocooned. He lunged at Megan, accidentally knocking a lever on the machine that sent a powerful blast towards the two golden cocoons. Everything then seemed to happen in slow motion. Chris had heard the noise and light. Abandoning the cows to Bruce, he fled back to the milking parlour. Matt was standing in shock, his mouth hanging open. Megan looked like a wild animal, but neither of them moved. Chris got to the door just in time to see two cocoons glowing gold and flickering. They started to hatch. He looked around in bewilderment. He hadn't seen Cameron and Rosie at all, so he had no idea what had just happened.

The lever Matt had knocked was capable of enhancing certain features—to make the animals more resilient, give more milk, provide more meat—although the farmer hadn't designed it to do specifically that. He had been working on a form of sonic ultrasound because by dramatically changing the size of his herd twice daily, the cattle did initially seem weakened by it. He was trying to reverse the effects of this. He had studied electro-physics at university, when he met a beautiful farmer's daughter. He had given everything up to marry her and had run the farm with her when her parents passed away. The power he had created was indescribable.

CHAPTER FOUR

NATURE IS NOT TO BE INTERFERED WITH

—◄o►—

Rapidly changing and morphing Rosie and Cameron into cocoons and then blasting them with sonic rays had inadvertently altered their DNA. Even creating this tiny glitch in the genetic code was enough to start a rapidly unravelling genetic meltdown—the start of mutation. The farmer had cocooned the few snoops who had made the mistake of coming to the farm. He had never once tried to reverse them. As far as he had been concerned, he kept them as trophies. This was a whole new territory. They began to morph in front of Megan, Chris, and Matt. Not one of them moved. The pupae started to hatch, recognisable but somehow enhanced, with stunning features and giving off an iridescent sheen. They had both developed athletic shapes. They felt strong, quickly taking in everything in their surroundings. Their senses were sharper. They felt a tinge of electricity pass between them. Rosie caught Megan's eye, sensing she was about to run, so she jumped towards her and the machine in a blur. She knocked all three over in one movement. Cameron could now see the cable leading out to the milk storage room, that Megan had watched her father attach to the machine. He knew he needed to pull the power source out. The machine needed to be destroyed. Fast. He didn't bank on it having a powerful electric force field. He couldn't touch the machine, and it threw him back into the pit. He climbed out, followed the cable, found the plug, and pulled it out of the wall. The machine started vibrating. Within seconds, it was firing beams at random, hitting parts of the parlour and the gates and exploding most of the glass milk cylinders that were still partially filled from the start of the day's milking. A wooden beam came down next to Rosie. Cameron tried to grab her, but he electrocuted her. A look of pain shot across her face. "Get out, everyone. I'll deal with this," he shouted.

"No, Cam," Rosie ignored everything around her, and it seemed to slow everything down. She stood calmly. "We finish this together." She was, as ever, the leader.

Megan came round from the blast, and she saw Rosie and Cameron. Why couldn't they understand that she needed that machine? Her anger raged more. She would make the old man and anyone who got in her way pay. Cameron felt strong, powerful, and electric. He wanted that machine destroyed. He moved quickly and met Megan's eyes as he reached the machine. She ran forward to try to stop him. He tried to touch the machine, but again, he was pushed away by its magnetism. He couldn't understand. It was no longer attached to a power source.

"You've got the same polar energy as the machine," Rosie called. This was Megan's chance. She lunged forward in their moment of hesitation. The machine was vibrating more violently as Cameron tried to touch it again. It fired, with more light and noise following.

"No, Megan! Stop!" Matt had recovered. He saw Megan near the machine, and he just needed to stop her. He didn't know it was no longer plugged into a power source, and he didn't know she couldn't control it. He tried to lunge at her, but she fell, taking him with her. The beam hit them both at the same time. Almost immediately, they both developed into golden brown cocoons.

Chris wanted to run, but he was transfixed to the spot. He had sat up, remembering Rosie running at him. Had he really just witnessed this? He couldn't comprehend any of it. Rosie didn't take her eyes off him, ready if he did run. She realised that she was very fast, and her mental ability was acute.

"Cameron, why do you think we hatched and the farmer hasn't?" She questioned it why the other cocoons stayed in that form when they had developed into pupae. Cameron went over to the cocoons, which were warm, soft, and glowing. The farmer's was, too. He then touched the pupae that he and Rosie had gotten out of. They were leathery and pliable, but dark and had peeled like a skin.

"I guess the only thing to do is find out." He hesitated. Matt was in one of those, but he didn't know which one.

Chris spoke up, "I saw Matt aim at the farmer. He just brought his fist down on the machine. I think he pressed several things because he shrunk and you didn't. I didn't see what happened with you. I didn't even know you were at the farm. Matt and Megan haven't shrunk, but there was only one blast of light. When I heard the light and noise, I came running into the barn and heard a much deeper boom. You changed quickly, and I think Megan most likely pressed more than one control." He spoke so quickly that he hadn't paused for breath.

As he gulped for air, Rosie nodded. "All the cocoons in the shed are like the farmer's. They have been shrunk afterward. Megan didn't shrink us. She would have known which button that was. Great meeting someone who wants to kill you but not shrink you! No gratitude. Cameron, it seems you can't touch the machine. You will only make it unstable again, I guess, if you go near it? We need to figure what to do to get Matt and Megan out safely. I think we should get some of the cocoons from the barn and try things on them first. I know it sounds harsh, but for all we know, they may be dead. It's got to be worth a shot?"

The three looked at each other in silence. How could any of them have guessed that they would be dealing with a situation so surreal. Chris was always dependable, and he had always been a little in the shadow of Cameron and Matt. They were always the centres of attention. Chris was a little more devious. He found ways of fitting in with exceptional politeness and charm. He was also really smitten with Rosie, though he never told the others. There was something in Megan that frightened him. She could be spontaneous, yet not in a good way. He realised that she had been through too much. She had turned on them. Nagging at the back of his mind was the sheer power of that machine, though. He really had an edginess that it was something he couldn't discuss with Cameron or Rosie. He needed Matt. So he squashed his greed and went with Rosie to collect the cocoons from the shed. They headed across the yard towards the shed, witnessing a strange sight. Two hundred cows had no idea what to do with themselves. The brief confusion that resulted after their enlargement and the lack of routine was too much for them. They eventually had found their way back to the smell of the farm and stood waiting. Being cows wasn't exactly hard; it just required the basics in life. Like all species, they needed routine and conformity even if they weren't aware of it consciously. A cow loves her calf as much as any human loves her child. The constant calling to reassure their calves, the calves wagging tails, happily suckling their mother's milk is all hormones, DNA, genetics, cells, and enzymes working together to produce a continuing line of life. Humans complicate the equation, to a degree. Even so, Rosie, with her new acute intelligence, couldn't help but extrapolate their lives and finally saw how amazing the natural world really was. It made her more determined to get Matt and Megan back, free the cocooned people and the farmer if possible, and then destroy the machine. She could see so much in her head, and life's balance was fragile enough without the aberrations of life Megan's father had created. She didn't say what she was thinking out loud, and she could tell Chris was struggling with the scenario. They made it into the shed, and the cows automatically followed them. The cows started to fill the shed, pulling and munching at the hay bales. There wasn't enough space for all of them, but as Rosie and Chris left, Chris noticed another store barn a short ways up. He asked Rosie to take the cocoons to Cameron, and he would try to house the cows before joining them in the parlour. His farming life was in his heart. He couldn't leave the cattle cold and hungry. He managed to get the cows into the barn next to the shed, with Bruce's help. He took several bales of hay back from the shed for them. His stomach rumbled, and he figured it must be lunchtime.

He decided to pop his head around the parlour door. "Cam, Rosie?" he called. "Are you still here?" Rosie was setting up the machine, plugging the huge cable back in, and Cameron was trying to figure how to turn all the milking equipment off.

"Hey Chris, you know about this. Can you help me?"

Chris replied, "We need something to eat and drink. Unlike you two, I'm not some super-powered freak." It was the first time they had mentioned the changes they had been through, as none of them knew what had really happened.

"Chris, get over here and do your stuff. It doesn't matter what has happened. We are all going to put this right. That is what mates are for! I will head to the farmhouse and see what food there is." Rosie shot him a filthy look. He shrugged and gave Chris a high five. He quite liked this new feeling, this strength and agility. Underneath, though, he had fallen in love with Megan the first time he had met her. As he went up to the farmhouse, he pondered what pain she must have been in. Lost in his thoughts, it was only Bruce barking at him that made him focus.

"Dog, you made me jump. You hungry?" His confidence meant the guard dog befriended him immediately. Bruce wasn't ever capable of being a guard dog anyway. He looked at Cameron, and it made him shiver. He was trying to tell him something. He had never had a dog—only cats that were much less loyal. He was surprised just how good this dog was with a complete stranger. He entered the farmhouse, which lacked a woman's touch, although he could see some beautiful paintings and needlework framed on the walls. The chairs were all a deep, dark brown leather, with thick tartan throws. He could smell the lingering of log smoke from the dead embers in the huge fireplace. Bruce nudged him. Cam stopped taking in Megan's home. There was nothing here for a child. How cruel had her father been to change her. He followed Bruce, not quite getting why, but sensing it was the right thing to do. Bruce was a sheep dog, after all. He knew from Chris chatting about his dog just how intelligent they were. They entered a big, stone-floored kitchen that worn but homey. He managed to procure some meat and bread, as well as a couple of apples. He threw some meat on the floor for Bruce that was gone in an instant. "Sorry, boy. This is all I could find. We all need to eat. If we have anything left, it is yours." As he ventured back to the milking parlour, Bruce followed him closely.

Encapsulated in their cocoons, the farmer's victims, the farmer, his daughter, and Matt were in a weird suspended animation. Cocoons are a capsule of life, and they were protecting all of them.

They were warm and floating, as if in a dream. They had no idea of anything else.

After the much-needed meal, Chris managed to collect some milk from the tank. None of them had realised how thirsty they were.

"Cam, do your fancy zapping on me soon so I can be like you guys. I feel a bit left out!" He was only half joking.

"Mate, we need to work out how to get everyone out of the cocoons. We don't know what Megan pressed. I am thinking it was guess work, as she sure didn't know about this machine before." Cameron was a little anxious. He understood Chris was normal, yet he and Rosie had evolved. Chris still wasn't completely sure of the enormous scale of what they could be dealing with.

"Chris, when we know it is safe, don't worry: We will help you. After all, you didn't try to kill either of us." He wasn't sure he meant it, but it reassured Chris.

Between the three of them, with Bruce lolling over the side of the milk parlour pit watching, they placed two of the cocoons in the pit. It lowered the odds of the rays scattering around the parlour as they had done earlier.

"Cam, stay *away* from the machine" Rosie insisted. "Now that it is plugged in, it could harm any of us with the magnetism." Rosie, yet again, was the leader. Chris stood behind Rosie, while Cam went and sat with his new friend, Bruce. Rosie pressed the button that had she thought enlarged things. The cocoons, still glowing gold, became full-sized. She then moved a lever, but no boom or changes visibly happened.

Chris intervened, "From where I could see Matt, he was pushing something down here, although I wasn't watching that closely," he mumbled.

"You know, Chris, you are a smart guy. Go for it. Like we said, we have to try anything." Rosie seemed rather confident. She looked at him and smiled. For the first time, she saw him—really saw him. She had all this newfound power and ability, but Chris didn't. He felt himself blush.

"Trust me on this one, then," Chris said. His heart was racing in his throat. He had no idea what he was about to do. He moved a lever and shut his eyes. The cocoons started to darken and pupate. The three of them watched anxiously. Two young men emerged from the pupae, with the athletic build Cameron and Rosie now had. They looked bewildered for a few seconds. Cam, Matt, and Chris prided themselves on wearing the right trends. These guys were wearing clothes they didn't even recognise, and they were different from anyone they had ever seen. The two looked at each other and then at Rosie. The younger man referred to her as Megan.

"What have you done, Megan?" He started to change, and you could see his body morphing and expanding. It was as though he was stretching after all the years he had been imprisoned. Something in his eyes changed colour. Cameron and Rosie saw it immediately, leapt in unison, and pulled Chris down between them. Chris had the sense to stay put. The other man was much, much older. His body was slowly peeling open, with large tendrils expanding out of his body. They didn't dare move. What Rosie had done by pressing the wrong button was to further destabilise the genetic code. In that few moments, both people were protected inside the cocoon during the critical stage of development. Chris had then managed to get them to pupate. Rosie realised that at least the monster in front of her must have been in that cocoon for a very long time. Mutations don't happen overnight, and the machine had somehow accelerated this. Hoping that Cameron and she were quick enough to outguess them, she thought quickly. They also needed to save Matt and Megan. Rosie had felt the jolt of electricity that passed through her when Cameron had tried to grab her hand. There was no way she could let him carry Chris. Cameron had to distract the two men so she could get Chris out of the way. Cameron nodded, for he already knew what she was thinking. Cameron lurched forward, hoping that he could stun the men with his electric force. Rosie pushed Chris behind the milk tank.

"Stay here!" she said. She headed back behind the machine. She aimed the machine at the men to shrink them, but Cameron was fighting with both of them. It seemed they both had other strengths. What was it that Megan's father had done to make this machine so powerful? She was genuinely scared. Instead, she risked everything, pointed the machine at the two cocoons still in the pit, and turned them into pupae. She just hoped that Matt and Megan would see sense. Cameron, in the meantime, was just fending off the two recently morphed creatures. He vaguely recognised the man with dark hair man and black eyes. He racked his brain while keeping them in the pit with repeated electric shocks. He understood how it must feel to be a trapped animal getting shocked by humans. He felt angry at his own race, angry at Megan's father, and angry at Megan for turning on them. As his anger exponentially increased, his electric force gathered more energy. He could see these mutations in front of him. Would this happen to him too? Without realising, he omitted a strong wave of force and knocked both mutations out instantly. Luckily, he was in the pit, so the concrete walls contained the force. Rosie took no time in cocooning them before shrinking them.

"Chris," called Rosie "We need you to put these guys somewhere safe." As reluctant as he was, he was given both cocoons, unconscious miniature freaks of nature, to find somewhere to contain them. It was time to man up. He could see that Rosie was looking at him proudly, so he slipped out of the parlour to the shed where the all-too-familiar bird cage was.

Meanwhile, Megan and Matt had metamorphosed. Their pupae started to split. A pale-skinned beauty stepped out, glistening and shimmering just as Rosie had. Cameron did a double take and took a sharp breath. Matt followed from his pod. Both looked amazing. Cameron and Rosie now understood how they must have looked, all resplendent and stunning. Cameron was almost overawed. Megan, with her super-fast brain ability, locked the remaining cocoon in the pit, as well as Cameron and Rosie standing defensively in front of them. Why was her father still a cocoon? She wanted to kill him, and she now felt incredibly light and flexible. She couldn't describe it, but she knew she could do anything she wanted. Matt, on the other hand, felt weak. He collapsed to the floor of the pit, ashen, barely able to breathe. Megan wasn't interested in any of them. She leapt sideways and picked up the tiny cocoon. She was gone. Cameron and Rosie ran to Matt. He was barely conscious.

"Rosie, what do we do? Why isn't he like the rest of us?"

Rosie reminded him, "They were hit with one bolt at the same time. Maybe everything transferred to Megan? I don't know. We need to get Matt safe and then work out what to do with this machine." As usual she was the one taking charge. Cameron never argued with her, for she was always right. "We need to warn Chris.

Megan is somewhere. She is dangerous to him, more than she is to us."

Cameron asked Rosie, "Can I take Matt and you find Chris?" Rosie looked at him incredulously. "Is there is nothing you haven't learned? Honestly! This isn't a good situation, but in case you failed to notice, anything you touch seems to get electrocuted or pushed away from you!"

Cameron was frustrated. He needed to help his friends. Rosie said, "Look, I can carry Matt. I'm strong enough. I will get him in the shed. I doubt that with all her bad memories, Megan would even consider going in there. Besides, she knows the machine is in here. You stay here and protect this machine. We still have to revive her father, regardless of what he has done. We have a duty to finish what we started. I've already told you. We can hold her off from the machine, because with you next to it, it becomes unstable. Megan can't risk getting in the way. She's not stupid. Stay put. I will find Chris and get him to stay with Matt."

Unbeknown to any of them, Matt had indeed transferred some of his kinetic energy to Megan, but he had received something far more sinister: All her anger and hatred were fused into a part of her brain, and this emotion had been transferred to Matt. Matt could feel everything Megan could. The pain was intense.

This was the beginning of a very long battle.

CHAPTER FIVE

GENERATION OF AN
ULTIMATE CHOICE

The effects of the machine hadn't stopped. Its energy was still working on their genetic code, shaping their DNA. They kept evolving, something none of them would have even guessed. Nature evolves over time, but the machine kept stimulating changes far more quickly.

None of them realised what was happening. It was deep within their cells. Their genetic codes were responding in part to their deeper emotions and perceptions.

Megan has morphed into a stunning young woman. Her clothes fit her like a glove. She was almost overpowering. Her whole persona was strong. She felt amazing. She had yet to feel any sense of fear or remorse. The machine had sensed her creativity and embraced it. Rosie, due to her kind, gentle nature, morphed into a beautiful young woman so clever that she was nearly a goddess. In her transformation, she shone with the most earthy yellows and greens moulded to her body. Clothes? It was more mother nature dressing her. Her red hair complemented her. She was a leader. She had strength in her mind no one could match. Cameron had evolved, too. He believed in himself. This was reflected in his metamorphism. He was fast and powerful and had foresight. He cared for his friends, and he still felt a sense of loyalty to all of them. He was their protector. Nagging at the back of his brain was fighting a love for Megan. Matt had taken the short straw. Because of his clash with Megan's anger, he developed reptilian-like scales. They were stunning. He had become red, black, orange, and white in human form. He had quick reflexes, but it was all built on anger. He was hungry for prey.

Chris was the only human left. He was a striking young man regardless. He knew the machine was important. He felt jealous of the others. He knew he had to do something to help, but he couldn't fathom what to do next.

They were exaggerated versions of themselves. It developed those genes to their full potential. Megan's father hadn't realised what he created. He had only tried to look after his stock.

Cameron heard commotion in the shed. He didn't want to leave the machine, though. He knew Megan would be back. The battle in the shed was intense. Matt was weak, but he had such quick reflexes that he managed to hide himself and Chris as Megan and Rosie met head on. Neither of them realised how powerful they were.

Megan and Rosie were locked in combat. Neither of them cared about the consequences. There was an underlying jealousy between them. They attacked each other, yet every time they touched, they evolved further. Their genes mutated again. Rosie's brain was far superior, and she knew she had to stop Megan. Something at the back of her mind remembered Megan's father mentioning multiplication. If she could get the machine to replicate herself, she could overcome Megan.

Matt could see that Megan was powerful with anger, and he could feel exactly what she was going through. He needed to distract her. He needed to help Rosie. They needed the machine. Matt said, "Chris, I'm not strong enough. Can you go to Cameron and move the machine here? I know it sounds crazy, but we need to stop the girls somehow. I can feel all the anger in Megan, and she isn't going to stop unless we stop her."

At this point, Chris was utterly terrified. He managed to sneak out of the shed. Megan and Rosie were so locked in combat, changing before his eyes. The two friends were now monsters trying to rip each other to pieces. They didn't notice him. He ran towards the milking parlour. Cameron was waiting for Megan. When Chris entered, he was wary. "Cameron? Are you here?" He called quietly. "Rosie and Matt need you and the machine. The girls are not themselves. It's horrible. I don't understand, but they are changing repeatedly.

"Chris, I'm here," Cameron reassured him.

No one realised that the farmer hadn't worked out how to divide. The machine could duplicate, but not deplete. The laws of science and nature had been altered. What would take thousands of years of through natural evolution was now taking seconds. Their powers increased. Cameron couldn't touch the machine. He found that he could move it with Chris next to him. Chris needed changing to survive this.

Cameron said, "Chris, we need you to be like us. Do you trust me enough?' Cameron knew he was doing the right thing.

Chris was already aware of enough. "To be fair, Cam, yeah. Just hope I don't turn out like Megan!" He tried to be cool. He stood in front of the machine, eyes closed. Cameron knew what to press now. He understood that the machine developed someone whilst they were cocooned. Then, by stimulating pupation, he could bring Chris back in a new form. It was weird because Chris, although normal, stopped any of the negative magnetism that Cameron emitted. Cameron enveloped Chris in a golden brown cocoon. He then pushed the lever that resulted in pupation. He waited with anticipation. Before his eyes, Chris stepped out of the pod. He looked soft, as though he was putty. He was also stunning to look at. His short blonde-ginger curls shone, and his eyes were piercing. Cameron couldn't help thinking that this machine was a little Hitler-oriented, remembering his history lessons. He hadn't seen himself since his evolution.

"Chris, how do you feel?" Cameron asked. For some reason he couldn't understand, he felt stronger with Chris next to him. He felt drawn to him. Chris felt a wave of electricity as did Cameron. The current flowed between them. The two boys started to morph again.

How could this happen without the machine? Cameron and Chris evolved again. Because of the connection of electricity, both of them had developed the ability to stun anything with just a look. They were not aware of this at the time. They moved the machine though the parlour doors and across the yard towards the shed. It didn't need a power connection now: Cameron and Chris powered it through their bodies.

Rosie and Megan were also evolving further, so fast in combat that they had almost lost any human sense and feeling. The boys stood at the shed door, watching a tremendous display of colour, three-dimensional morphing, and two creatures they no longer fully recognised. Only the sleek black hair and the golden red curls gave away that these mutations were Megan and Rosie. Matt was still really weak, and he was watching in amazement. The girls had lost all sense and feeling of normality. Despite their intelligence, their bodies had mutated many times in mere minutes. They were locked in battle, not challenging what was happening. The jealousy and anger ran too deep in both of them.

Without realising, Chris and Cameron started the machine. They were both so engrossed and amazed at what was going on in front of them that their emotions rose and the machine fired. It spun round and fired constantly. All four of them were hit by the blasts. They were cocooned. Matt, hiding in the hay bales, lifted his head to see the glowing cocoons on the shed floor in front of him. He struggled to get up and saw his arms and legs for the first time. What an earth had happened to him? He was hungry, and he wanted to kill. Fighting his emotions, he knew he needed to do something. How could he reverse all this, and how could he help his friends?

The machine would not respond to him. He pressed every button and lever to no avail. He didn't want to leave the cocoons, but he had to go back to the milking parlour to get the cable. His head was racing: What did he need to do? He gathered the cable and looked around at the terrible mess. The parlour was destroyed. Pupae pods lay on the milk-drenched floor, and there was glass scattered everywhere. Where had Megan put her father's cocoon? He wondered. Heading back to the barn, he had no idea what he was going to do. He was deformed from a human state, and his fore and hind legs moved in unison. He was still quick and agile. His tongue tasted his surroundings, and his capacity to think had been enhanced. Despite the mutations, he was a gentle soul. He had to fight Megan's hatred and anger, as well as the burning desire to rip flesh. He was cold, and it slowed down his metabolism enough to quench his hunger for now. He had evolved into a massive, stunning reptilian creature. He was six feet long, at least. His black and white scales glistened, and his muscles clenched. He still knew he had to do something, and animal instinct had kicked in.

Matt finally set up power to the machine. Somehow, deep within him, he managed the dexterity to stand on his hind legs and concentrate his being to do what was necessary. He still had little inkling of what it was doing to their genetic codes. He wanted to pupate Cameron first, for he knew his soul was completely pure. He was his best friend, and he could trust him regardless of what happened. Even in his mutated form, he had a sense of loyalty that overrode the hatred Megan had passed to him. He managed to point the machine at the furthest pupae, thinking that was where Cameron had been when he had briefly lifted his head above the bales. A deep boom shook the shed. The furthest cocoon did exactly as he knew it would. It began to transform and pupate. It wasn't Cameron that stepped out of the peeling pupae pod. It was a dark-haired, beautiful monster. He felt her anger and power. Megan was dangerous. He decided to shrink her, but she knew exactly what he was thinking. Their minds were locked together. She was beside him in a second. She didn't need to speak, for he understood what she wanted. He stood in front of the machine and waited. Megan's mind had overpowered his. He was going to be just like her. They would fight the world. It didn't dawn on him that he was no longer human. Megan was beautiful. He just felt the need to survive. He knew she was going to change him. His will had been overpowered.

Megan was a blistering force. Despite her evolution, her head was very much in control.

She was the queen bee. She pressed the lever to change Matt, and he cocooned as expected. However, the link between Cameron and Chris meant the magnetism pulled the machine towards their cocoons. It started vibrating as Megan tried to stop it. She pulled the cable out, but it was too late. It started blasting beams and spinning again. It hit all five of them several times, and all five of them shrank.

Looking down, the farmer watched and laughed. The strength of the blast Cameron and Chris had given the machine had also rejuvenated his cocoon. He had pupated and then hatched. He had changed. His love and grieving had made him softer, but his bond with his flesh and blood was stronger.

However, he was still a collector, and he liked his trophies. He had evolved into a black and white corvid, a type of magpie but in mainly human form. His eyes darted everywhere; he had watched the initial fighting in front of him with shock. He saw what his daughter had become. He was fascinated.

Matt morphed into a creature very similar to Megan. His theatrical side was enhanced. He remained a myriad of colours and scales, and he was fearless.

Rosie's pupa opened. She had evolved into a fighting alpha warrior. She was prickly, and dark green spines covered her flesh due to her jealously. She still moved gracefully and quickly. It was as though nature was trying to give her something. Her heart was good. She sensed she needed to destroy evil. She had yet to realise that she could slow time (at the speed of sound).

Barely recognisable, Cameron's blonde floppy hair just defined a creature of immense power. He had retained his electrical ability. Chris too was changed; his body was muscular and barely human. He felt a surge of passion and anger at the same time. He and Rosie locked eyes.

The five of them began to duplicate. The numbers kept increasing exponentially. In time, there were thousands of morphed interpretations, vaguely resembling humans. Each time they multiplied, certain aspects of their emotions and need to battle, kill, or survive altered. The battle was indescribable. The genetic code was so altered that no human structure remained. The only thing that left intact was instinct.

The five of them mutated exponentially, and the mutations increased to the region of 78,125; 15,625 of each of them. They had all changed so frequently at each conflict that it was a blur. It was a most vibrant colourful blur, a constant change in the dynamics with a fight for which they had lost the reason. The only thing that slowed any of them was a vital flaw in the machine. Each of them were multiplying and mutating, but they couldn't divide. Rosie and Cameron's mutated selves fought against Megan and Chris, as the two were in symmetry. Chris had slowly come to fight with Megan and Matt. At this one moment, 15,625 of each of them raged against each other. They evolved to such a level that they began to second guess each others' moves. Each would start a battle, but the others were already prepared. It was an impossible struggle. Time after time, they evolved to a greater level and became the most amazing monsters combined with immense power. They didn't achieve anything.

Their souls were still intact, shaping the creatures into which they mutated. The connection between Megan and Matt meant that the anger ran through his veins as deeply as hers. Their creatures were dark, cruel, and aggressive. Chris was their tail guard, the dog at their feet. His confusion meant he didn't evolve as quickly. He partly wanted them all to want the same thing. That was his weakness. They continued to fight for a reason no one could remember.

CHAPTER SIX

HUMAN NATURE

◄O►

The five tiny monsters hadn't noticed the farmer leering above them; they were engrossed deep in battle. He had contained them in a large glass terrarium he had used to keep tadpoles as they turned into froglets when he was a teenager. He still watched with fascination at the mutations. The only reason he could recognise was Megan because her clothing was part of her mutation. He was drawn to silver. Whatever she morphed into had shades of purple and silver. He recognised Rosie from her green and yellow streaks. The boys were less defined. He secured the lid and called Bruce. He needed sleep. It had been a busy few days, but he smiled contentedly. He had his daughter back. Forever.

The battle raged. Everything intersected, and war intensified between the mutants. Each time they met, raging against each other, they mutated again.

Cameron realised deep down that this wasn't going anywhere. His 15,625 selves felt an urge. He needed to go backward, and he needed only his friends. His thoughts about Megan surged through him, all of him. Forgetting he had electricity running through him, the thoughts he had caused an atomic bomb like explosion. It knocked the other mutants down in an instant.

Cameron needed to get to Megan. He realised what had happened. His stun would only last briefly. He knew they all knew each other's plans. Until now. His feelings for his friends and Megan had taken over. All of him searched, but there were too many stunned creatures to even guess which one was the original Megan. He knew he had to leave her a message, something to reverse things.

Sure enough, his electric current only stunned everyone for a short while. Megan pre-empted the next strike. She and Matt blocked the onslaught of Rosie and Cameron. Chris took up their flank but hesitated. Luckily, Rosie had perfected the capacity to slow time briefly. It was long enough to show Megan a few words. Cameron had managed to think ahead by a few milliseconds. As Megan started mutating again, she saw it. His words stopped her in her tracks. "I love you," he said. The feeling inside her was so powerful that it stopped her anger long enough. She started to realise her anger was about being kept a prisoner. Her whole life had been controlled, and her father had treated her the same as he did his animals. Even Bruce was treated better than her. Her emotions ran deep, despite the changes to her form. Little did she know that they had evolved and mutated so much that it was not going to be an easy task to undo. Cameron had somehow altered her mutation.

Megan and Cameron met, all 31,250 of them. It just happened, and they felt drawn to each other. By meeting, their collision of powers changed everything. They watched it happen, and sand poured from the mouths of their mutations in front of them. Each mutation went through all their mutations in reverse. They were eventually met with copies of their human selves in sand, which then fell to the ground. Dust. There was just the two of them, not recognisable in form, but somehow Cameron and Megan embraced. It was no longer war between the two of them. Love had conquered her demons for now.

They had no idea that they were trapped in a glass tank. The brief memory loss after a blast from the machine meant that as they were shrunk, Megan's father had been able to scoop all five of them up. He was first rate at dealing with miniatures.

Between them, Cameron and Megan realised they had to put good thoughts and feelings everywhere. They had second guessed moves before and blocked each other at every turn. Now their efforts were combined. Instead of anger, they both generated happy feelings. As a result, the mutations of Chris, Rosie, and Matt were surrounded by red and pink light. The strength of the electrical connection between Cameron and Chris intensified. He met Chris head on, all of him. They were muscular leathery bat like beings, with large eyes and intense speed. With Megan next to him, pale, shimmering, and elegant, Cameron still felt he could stop this. They needed to stop this. Chris saw Megan in front of him. She was glittering as though made of diamonds, and he was entranced.

"Chris," she said quietly. "Stop." As she spoke, thousands of stars spanned around them. She was happy and had generated the stars. Cameron focused on Chris, and he extended his electric field as far as he could. Chris felt it, and he felt that Cameron was his brother. He could feel the pull of the magnetism. Chris watched as his fellow mutations turned to sand. The multiple mutations and morphs reversed before their eyes. It didn't matter. He wanted to see Rosie, and his memory was returning. Cameron and Megan had something beyond the control of mutation—the ability to love. Deep down, they both started to feel more human. Chris began to feel purposeful, as well.

Rosie had been keeping Matt occupied in combat. The combined 31,250 of them changed and outwitted each other without achievement. Suddenly, they were glittering, and regardless of how far they had morphed, Matt and Rosie couldn't help but stall. What was going on? They were all transformed into mutations barely recognisable as themselves, but they were reflecting light against each other! They couldn't see as the mirrored light bounced off all of them. It gave Megan, Cameron, and Chris time to gain control. Cameron blasted his electric ray again. He watched as the thousands of mutants exploded in front of them, turning again into sand after going through each mutation in reverse. The air became filled with fireworks generated from the implosion.

Cameron and Megan had joined in heart and mind. All their surroundings exploded with colour and shape. The intensity between them morphed them again. They seemed more human, but only marginally. Chris was mutating differently. He was becoming more porous, with threads of tissues and blood vessels. Rosie and Matt stood together and looked up at the amazing display. Matt, as ugly a monster he had become, put his clawed foreleg in one of Rosie's tentacles. Neither resembled themselves at all, yet deep within, something had changed again. Friendship and love had prevailed. Around them was a deep layer of dust.

It was far from over. Their genetic code had been so destructed that they began to mutate and multiply again.

The battle was far from over.

CHAPTER SEVEN
THE QUANTUM LEAP

—◄O►—

The farmer hadn't been completely honest with Megan or her friends. His wife had been dying. He had originally tried to build the machine to save her—to cocoon her until such a day he could heal her and bring her back.

After several years, still absorbed in grief, he had tried to bring her back. The machine he was working on developing meant that he had kept her frozen in time, safe. He wanted her. He spent many lonely days and nights wishing he could hold her and watch her laugh. Megan was still so young. He developed the machine further for the farm. That part was true. One day, he couldn't hold it in, and he pupated his wife's cocoon. When it hatched, he hadn't managed to keep his wife as he knew her. The machine had not been powerful enough

Bruce became his faithful companion. His wife's deepest love and affection had evolved. Her emotions and care took control of her genetic code as she was developing inside the pupa. The farmer wouldn't accept it, and he couldn't comprehend what had happened. He struggled to acknowledge her change of form. In sadness, though, trying to block the thoughts of the transformation and his own guilt, he welcomed this dog into his home. He called her Bruce. In his head, his wife had gone. He gave the dog a masculine name to help. Bruce had been his only morph, for he cocooned anyone who dared trespass or nose. He never touched a cocoon again once it was made. He had lied to himself so often that he eventually forgot the truth, but his wife's memory was still with him, too deeply engrained. Bruce had retained his wife's intellect, yet it was her love that kept her close to her husband and daughter. She had never morphed again.

Now, the farmer had changed. He was still keeping his trophies, but his conditioning was to tend to his farm. He knew deep down that he had Megan and his wife with him. The day after he had collected the five into the terrarium, he got up and continued as normal. It was very similar to the monotonous routine of his cattle, not that he noticed the similarity.

Inside the terrarium, the battle continued with a different reason. Chris, Cameron, Matt, Megan, and Rosie had all briefly come to the same conclusion. With the damage done, they had all mutated again, but each was trying to support the others. Each time they tried to interact, they morphed and mutated. There were an infinite number of possibilities, and there was no stopping the process.

Almost all living organisms carry DNA, the main constituent of the chromosomes and the king of molecules. It twists and turns inside cells and carries all the genetic information. It is able to replicate itself and change its sequence of molecules to determine each individual, but it always retains some individual characteristics that have been hereditary. Hence, no matter how many times they mutated, they still had part of their original genetic makeup. Each could vaguely recognise each other while trying to fight the scientific damage that had been done. They had, however, lost the ability to speak. Evolution doesn't always favour the right genes, especially at the speed at which they were evolving.

Cameron had inadvertently created a severe imbalance in nature's equilibrium when he used his electromagnetic energy to destroy all of their previous mutations. The terrarium was their prison, but it was a contained, restricted environment. Inside it, they were changing without any of them realising it. By rapidly destabilising equilibrium, the particles of subatomic energy from the dust of the mutants escaped into the atmosphere. These particles interacted with each other on an entirely different level. Quantum physics still held, even in this world.

The turbulence that followed was almost immeasurable. With the release of electrons from the destabilisation of the mutant dust, a wave of electric energy exchange occurred. Some of the electrons pulled towards each other, creating a symmetry that resulted in their lining up and producing an intense magnetic field. Other electrons developed during their altering space and spinning coordinates. Uncontrolled by anything else, they began to oppose each other. This was similar to the effect Cameron had on the machine. He hadn't been able to go near it without Chris. Together, they had effectively lined up their energy without realising it.

Cameron and Chris knew that the human body generally had the same number of protons to electrons and that the protons were paired with neutrons. Neither of them had thought that life could be so changed by DNA mutation and destruction. They were seeing things on an entirely new level. The situation was dire.

"I can always tell when I don't have enough protons in my body because I feel really negative." Cameron had to joke. Nobody heard his thoughts, or so he thought. He couldn't see, but Chris had heard him in his head. They watched as the atmosphere changed. Both of them could feel the body of electrons fighting against them. They joined hands, knowing they were a stable unit now. No subatomic particles could affect them unless they joined to them, making both of them more powerful.

Megan had mutated until she became diamond-like. She had superlative physical qualities and was effectively unbreakable. Her ability to disperse light in many different colours meant she radiated a constant array of colours. Additionally, she developed the capacity to withstand any of the electrical fields being created around her, just like a diamond.

Rosie and Matt had developed powerful perceptions. Rosie was capable of time dilation, something only ever seen on long space missions. She aged and changed less than the others whilst mutating. The mirrors were still there. Regardless of the number of times she and Matt evolved, part of their bodies still influencing their power. A light pulsed, bouncing between their mirrors. Rosie affected time more now than when they were separated. When a light pulse hit, it created a mirror image of light backward and forward between them. Until they moved apart, the light never stopped reflecting, as strong as it was at the start. Together, Rosie and Matt slowed the mutations among all five of them long enough to communicate with Cameron, Chris, and Megan. The light pulse from Matt and Rosie generated a rainbow above them. It was a sign of hope.

The destabilisation of the dust particles caused an energy exchange, resulting in further magnetic fields being created around them. The vibrations set off electromagnetic waves, pulsing at a low frequency barely audible to them all. Above the five of them, strange cloudlike shapes started to develop.

Effectively, they had created their own ionosphere, full of free subatomic particles energised by Megan's radiation of light. The pulsing electromagnetic waves caused the subatomic particles to react. Heat concentrated above and reflected back to the ground, causing it to space quake. The five of them braced themselves together, and by touching, all five mutated again. This enhanced their abilities to adjust to another adverse situation. Balance was paramount, so their centres of gravity changed to reflect this. Their skeletons and muscle structure developed so that their bodies were lower to the ground and more streamlined, almost like a flea or a flat fly.

No one could fully understand the changes around them. They still didn't know they were in a sealed glass container. Everything that happened was contained and inadvertently had a knock-on effect. The atmosphere was becoming moist, and condensation was trickling down the insides of the terrarium. Each breath they took made it worse. The energy flow created by Cameron, Chris, and the destabilised dust releasing the subatomic electrons was still creating continual electromagnetic waves. The cool drops of condensation fell above them and interfered with the flow. The warm humid air around them collided with the cool moist air above causing the remaining dust beneath them to start swirling about. The energy from the warm, moist air was fuel to move the dust below and the cloudlike shapes above them. A hurricane was born.

Cameron and Megan embraced, trying to stabilise each other from being ripped up into the air. There was nothing to hold onto. Somewhere deep in his subconscious, Chris remembered his physics lessons. He pulled Rosie and Matt towards him, dragging them into the eye of the hurricane before it gathered more speed. They watched as Cameron and Megan disappeared into the revolving dust. The three below were helpless, regardless of how powerful their mutations had become.

Everything they did now was based on telepathic communication. There was no need for words. Megan could feel Cameron trying to hold her. She could feel the electric rays bouncing off her, but she could also feel the heat around her travelling through her body. She was aware she was now unbreakable and gripped Cameron tightly. She knew she had to save him.

The fact that Cameron and Chris were separate caused a massive surge in polarisation. All the free subatomic ions in the hurricane cloud started to be attracted to one or the other of them, effectively reducing the power of the hurricane. There was a marked drop in energy flow despite the heat. Moist, cool condensation generated in the container. Cameron and Megan started falling rapidly. Megan instinctively twisted underneath him. He didn't quite understand but read her thoughts. She was as hard as a diamond. Nothing but another diamond could damage her. She braced his collision well, though they still managed to crack the floor beneath them.

The hurricane absorbed the oxygen from the terrarium's atmosphere, creating a dangerous environment for all of them. None of them could breathe for long if the hurricane continued, though they didn't know this. As the oxygen levels fell, the five of them started to evolve again to differing degrees stimulated by the increase in carbon dioxide in their blood streams. The creation of an anaerobic environment clearly favoured the development of their DNA to develop quickly to adapt to these inhospitable conditions. As is the nature of biological changes, the five of them did not evolve exactly the same. With oxygen depletion in the air, their bodies transformed to utilise the atomic bound oxygen inside their own cells. The elements that had been bound to the oxygen, nitrogen and sulphur, had become displaced. The nitrogen became a free inert gas, dissolving into their blood streams in the compressed atmosphere of the terrarium.

The sulphur, however, combined with hydrogen in their body tissues and made a dangerous chemical. They started to release a foul-smelling, slightly yellow gas whenever they breathed. The air became more polluted with each breath they took. As the dangerous chemical started to concentrate in the atmosphere, they all began to feel weak and nauseous. Their DNA failed to mutate because of the imbalance in chemicals affecting their bodies.

They produced more hydrogen sulphide because they were breathing anaerobically and then inadvertently breathing it in, which was in a vicious cycle. Cameron's senses were weakening; he was forgetting all about Megan and his friends. Chris, too, having already been weakened by the loss of connection with Cameron, felt very drowsy. He started to lose consciousness. Megan felt was uneasy and irritable. She was so tired, but she was far more resistant than the others. She held onto Cameron closely, but knew she couldn't do anything. Somewhere deep from inside, her emotions re-emerged. Remembering the hatred she once had, she wondered if this was what the monster who called himself her father wanted? Her thoughts helped her stay strong. Rosie and Matt had both collapsed. Neither of them could smell the foul odour around them, but their eyes were streaming with tears from the noxious gas. Rosie could feel her throat was tight, and she was struggling to breathe. Matt clung to Rosie but lost unconsciousness quickly.

Evolution of the genetic code enables creatures to survive better when prone to a natural exposure of hydrogen sulphide. Despite their rapid mutation, they hadn't been exposed to this poisonous, highly flammable gas before. All of them were suffering its toxic effects to varying degrees, each affected slightly differently.

Megan was thinking hard. She needed Cameron, and she knew he would be able to help her. She tried hard to connect with his mind, shocked at the wall building inside him. *I love you,* she screamed in her head. Cameron was jolted, and he felt his heart pounding and sensed someone holding his weak body. Megan. He fought the toxic effects of gas with all his remaining strength, and sparks flew from his fingertips.

The terrarium was already weakened by Megan and Cameron's fall. The hydrogen sulphide exploded, the terrarium shattered, and the blast threw all five weakened, mutilated bodies to the floor in the farmer's kitchen. It woke Bruce, who was actually Megan's mother, up from the dog basket. She went over, and her large wet nose sniffed at these weird creatures lying before her. Gently, she picked each one up in turn and carried them to the safety of her bed.